LITTLE ELEPHANT'S CHRISTMAS

LITTLE ELEPHANT'S CHRISTMAS

STORY BY HELUIZ WASHBURNE
PICTURES BY JEAN McCONNELL

LAUGHING ELEPHANT · MMIX

ORIGINALLY PUBLISHED BY ALBERT WHITMAN & COMPANY IN 1938.

ISBN13 978-1-59583-373-0

www.LAUGHINGELEPHANT.COM

LITTLE ELEPHANT was all excited. In a few days it would be Christmas. School was over and snow lay white and thick on the ground.

Many times each day the bell in the kitchen went ting-a-ling-a-ling and Little Elephant rushed to the door to see who was there. Sometimes it was the expressman who drove up in a truck and dumped a big box or two. Sometimes it was the postman who came up the path with a mail bag of little bundles swinging from his trunk.

There were long bundles, short bundles, flat bundles, round bundles, thin bundles, square bundles —bundles, bundles, bundles! And all of them were pasted over with bright red Christmas seals.

"Can't I open just one now?" teased Little Elephant. But Mother Elephant always said, "No, not till Christmas morning," and she piled them up in the hall. He looked at them, shook them, and wondered what was inside.

Little Elephant had saved his money and had bought Christmas presents for the family. He was pleased about the things he had chosen, and he often picked them up and looked at them.

This was a nice grey woolly trunk-warmer for Grandpa Elephant — poor Grandpa's nose was always cold. Little Elephant liked the bright red stripes around this one. Here was a lovely wide silver lace collar for Mother Elephant to make her look beautiful.

And this little bundle was a box of special paints for Father Elephant. He would use them to decorate his tusks. Father Elephant was very proud of his fine, long tusks.

At last came the day before Christmas. Wrapped in a large red and white checked apron, Mother Elephant was making the big Christmas pudding. Little Elephant watched her rub the butter and

This was a nice grey woolly trunk-warmer

sugar together, drop in the eggs, and pour in the rich brown molasses. Then she added the plump raisins, the nuts and the red cherries.

When it was all mixed she scooped it out onto a cloth and tied it up like a bag, put it in a huge kettle of water and set it on the stove to boil.

"Here, Little Elephant, you can scrape the bowl," she said. And that was exactly what Little Elephant had been waiting for.

Father Elephant came home with a big Christmas tree in his trunk.

"Oh, will it touch the ceiling?" cried Little Elephant when he saw it.

That night Father Elephant set up the tree and it *did* touch the ceiling. Little Elephant helped to trim it. Father Elephant strung the lights and then unrolled the big ball of shiny tinsel. Holding it on his tusks he threw big loops of it around and around the tree. Little Elephant hung up the bright balls and the silver stars.

Then Little Elephant very carefully opened a box of Christmas snow. It looked pretty and soft so he put the tip of his trunk in to feel it. Some of the

He threw big loops of it around and around the tree

snow slipped inside his nose and he gave a gentle "Whhoof." That stirred up some of the snowflakes and gave him a splendid idea.

Laying his trunk on the edge of the box he gave a mighty blow—"Pooh-ooh." The air was filled with a cloud of snowflakes and they fell down all over the green branches of the lovely Christmas tree.

"Now it is time to hang up your stocking and go to bed," said Father Elephant.

Little Elephant ran upstairs and came down waving in his trunk the biggest stocking he could find. When he had hung it beside the fireplace he went off to bed as good little elephants should.

Early the next morning Little Elephant galloped into his mother's room. "Merry Christmas!" he bellowed, "Merry Christmas!"

Mother Elephant sat up sleepily in her bed. Surely it couldn't be morning already. She rubbed her eyes and straightened her nightcap.

"Come on! Get up! I want to see what's in my stocking," Little Elephant cried, pulling at the covers.

"Brrr!" shivered Mother Elephant as she heaved

Little Elephant came down waving the biggest stocking he could find

herself out of bed and put on her snuggly red flannel robe.

In the next room Father Elephant was snoring loudly, "Ugghhhhhhhh-Zzzzzz! Uggghhhhhhhh-Zzzzzzzz!" Little Elephant ran in to wake him up. "Uggghhhhhh-Zzzzzzz," rumbled Father Elephant. The bed shook and the floor trembled while Father Elephant slept peacefully on.

Little Elephant had to see what was in his stocking, but he couldn't go down without Father Elephant. So he walked up to the bed on tiptoe and very gently blew in Father Elephant's big ear.

Father Elephant wiggled his ear and slept on. Little Elephant blew again, harder this time. Then Father Elephant flapped his big ear, gave a huge grunt, rolled over and woke with a snort. "Here, what's the matter?" he growled.

"Merry Christmas!" shouted Little Elephant.

Father Elephant opened his twinkly eyes, and out of the corner of one saw Little Elephant standing beside his bed. "Oh, it's you," he rumbled. "And what do you want at this time of the night? Go back to bed, you young rascal."

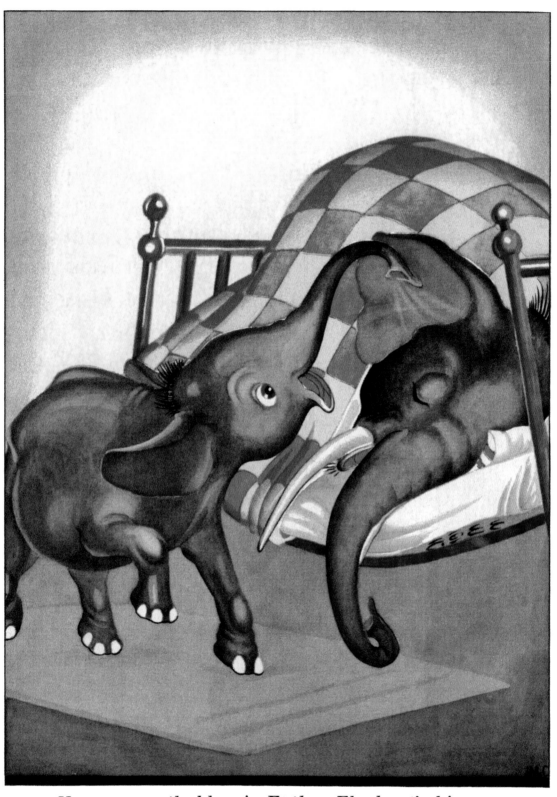

He very gently blew in Father Elephant's big ear

"It's morning and I want to see what's in my stocking," piped Little Elephant jumping up and down.

"Well, well, well," muttered Father Elephant as he tumbled out of bed and felt around on the floor for his big, round carpet slippers.

With all this noise, old Grandpa Elephant was soon awake. "What's the matter? Is the house on fire?" he called out in his squeaky voice and came tottering into the hall. He was still wearing his long pointed, black nightcap with the red tassel on the end.

Little Elephant had heard that Grandpa Elephant didn't have any hair on the top of his head. But he wasn't sure because Grandpa Elephant always wore a wig in the daytime. And at night he wore his nightcap so that he wouldn't catch cold.

Now they all started down the stairs. Little Elephant marched ahead, clatter - clatter - clatter. Mother Elephant, holding up her wrapper, padded softly behind, plop-plop-plop. Father Elephant lumbered along next, tromp-tromp-tromp, almost losing his carpet slippers at every step. At the end

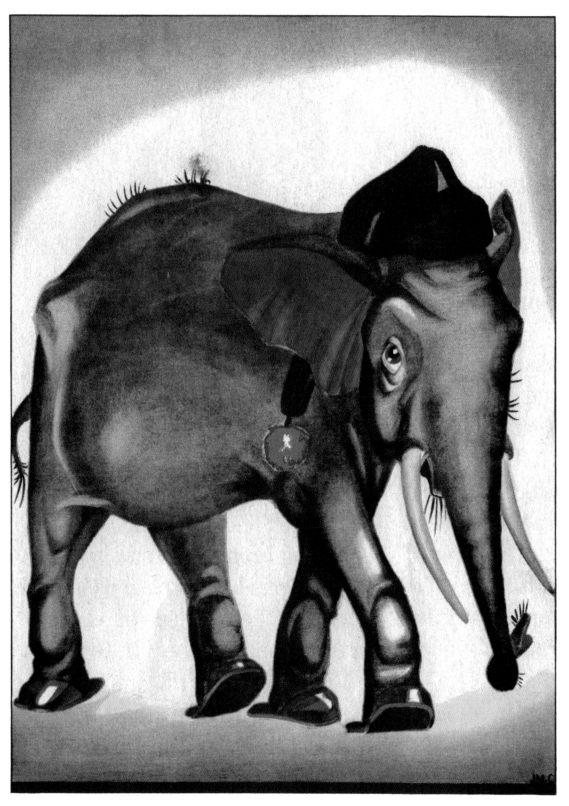

He was still wearing his long, pointed black nightcap

came Grandpa Elephant, shuffle-shuffle-shuffle.

"Ye-ey! Look at my stocking!" cried Little Elephant as he ran over to the fireplace. It was long and bumpy and full of queer bulges. He trotted back upstairs, waving the stocking in his trunk.

Then the rest of the family followed him and climbed up onto Father Elephant's large bed to watch Little Elephant empty his stocking.

He put in his trunk and brought out a big bunch of bananas. "Mmmm!" he cried, as he peeled one and popped it into his mouth. Then he peeled one for Father and one for Mother and one for Grandpa Elephant.

The next thing he pulled out was a wonderful brass trumpet. As soon as he had swallowed his banana Little Elephant wrapped his trunk around the horn and blew, "TOOT-toot! TOOT-toot!"

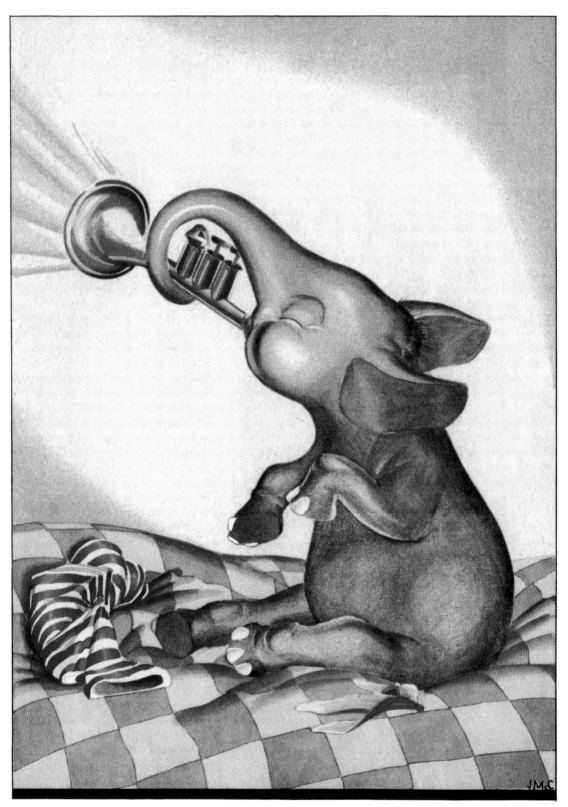

Little Elephant blew, "TOOT-toot! TOOT-toot!"

At the first blast Mother Elephant cried, "Oh dear," and pulled the covers over her head. "Eek!" piped Grandpa Elephant, and flapped his ears shut. "Ho-ho-ho!" laughed Father Elephant. He liked the horn and wanted to blow it himself.

Again and again Little Elephant poked his trunk down into his stocking and pulled out games and toys and red apples, and lollypops wrapped up in colored papers. His stocking grew thinner and thinner.

Now there was just one thing left, right in the very tiptoe of his stocking. He could hardly reach it. He wriggled and wriggled his trunk away down inside the long, empty stocking.

There—he had hold of the thing at last. What could it be? He saw Mother Elephant and Father Elephant winking at each other. Grandpa Elephant held the toe of the stocking while Little Elephant pulled out the package. He tore it open.

A wrist watch! A big, round, shiny brass wrist watch with a fine leather strap! Little Elephant bounced up and down on the bed when he saw it. Then he held it up to his ear, "Tick-tick-tick!" Yes,

A big, round, shiny brass wrist watch!

it was a real watch. Then he saw a little knob on top. "What's this for?" he asked.

But just at that second the watch went off with a sound like a fire gong. "Brrrrrr-rrrrrr!" rang the alarm. Little Elephant thought it would never stop. He looked so surprised that Mother and Father Elephant doubled up with laughter.

When breakfast was over Father Elephant gave everybody his presents from the big pile under the Christmas tree. Of course, Little Elephant got the most. But Father and Mother and Grandpa Elephant were as excited and happy as he was.

Grandpa said that his nose was cold right then, and so he pulled on his grey and red trunk-warmer.

Father Elephant went and stood before the mirror and painted his tusks so he would look beautiful for Christmas.

Mother Elephant proudly put on her silver lace collar and said she'd never felt so dressed up before.

One of the presents Little Elephant liked best was the funny game Grandpa Elephant gave him. In the box were a bunch of corks and a picture of a monkey with a hole cut out for his mouth.

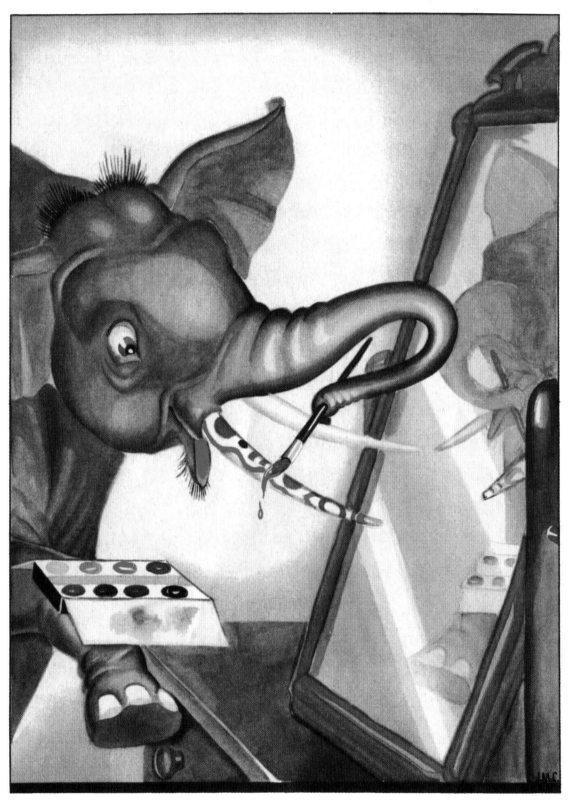

Father Elephant stood and painted his tusks

The trick was to shoot the corks into the monkey's open mouth. That was easy. Little Elephant took up a cork in the end of his trunk, aimed, and blew. Away shot the cork, poof! But it didn't hit the monkey. It caught Father Elephant in a tender place just behind the ear. That didn't please him at all.

When Father Elephant was settled down to his reading again Little Elephant tried once more. But just then Mother Elephant yawned. She wasn't used to getting up so early. And the cork landed plunk! right in her mouth. She coughed and gasped and Father Elephant thumped her on the back.

"Now, Little Elephant, you'll have to run outdoors and play," she sputtered as soon as she got her breath again.

When dinner was ready Mother Elephant called Little Elephant to come in. The table was sagging in the middle from all the food, and the good smells made Little Elephant's trunk quiver.

"Oh-oo!" said Father Elephant, sitting down at the head of the table in a great high-backed chair.

"Ah-aa!" sighed Mother Elephant as she dropped into a smaller chair at the other end.

She coughed and gasped

"Mm-mmm," murmured Grandpa Elephant, who settled into a comfortable chair with a cushion.

"Can I have a drumstick?" cried Little Elephant, as he climbed up onto his high stool. And then he looked at the bowl of soup in front of him and said, "Humph!"

He knew he must finish that soup before he could get any of the real dinner. So he dipped his trunk inside and gave a mighty suck, "Uuuuu-uuuuup!" Then he squirted it down his throat.

Mother Elephant looked at him and whispered, "Oh, Little Elephant! That's not polite."

When Little Elephant could see the pattern on the bottom of his bowl, he said, "Now, can I have my drumstick?"

"Yes, Little Elephant. But you must wait until the rest of us have finished our soup," said Mother Elephant.

Little Elephant waited and waited. Why did grown-ups have to talk so much?

At last Father Elephant began to serve. "Now here's a fine drumstick for you," he said.

Little Elephant ate one drumstick and then an-

He looked at the bowl of soup and said, "Humph!"

other and another and another, as well as all the other good things. Then Mother Elephant went out into the kitchen and came back with the Christmas pudding on a great silver tray.

Little Elephant sighed because he felt ready to burst and he didn't see how he could eat any pudding, and he'd been waiting all day for that pudding. So he got up and trotted around the table ten times to joggle down his turkey. He must make room for the Christmas pudding!

That afternoon when Little Elephant was tired of playing with all his toys and games, Mother Elephant said, "Come on into the kitchen, Little Elephant, and we'll have a taffy pull."

Now there was nothing that Little Elephant liked better than a taffy pull. Soon the big pot of candy was bubbling on the stove.

At last it was cooked enough and Mother Elephant poured the thick, sticky stuff onto a huge platter and set it outdoors. When it was cool she brought it in and scraped it all up into a ball.

"Now take hold, Little Elephant. It's ready to pull," she said.

So he got up and trotted around the table

Little Elephant buttered the end of his trunk so the candy wouldn't stick and he grabbed hold of the wad of taffy. It was hot but he held on and pulled, backing away from his mother, who was also pulling.

Soon the taffy stretched out into a thick rope between them. Then they looped it back together and pulled again. They had to work fast. Sometimes Little Elephant wasn't quick enough, and the taffy slipped off his trunk in long strings. Then he had a terrible time making it all stick together again.

When it was almost finished they went into the other room to show Father and Grandpa Elephant how it was coming. But Little Elephant had waited too long without pulling and now the taffy had begun to stick to his trunk. The more he tried to get it off, the worse it stuck, until a big wad of it was wrapped around his nose. He shook his trunk, he snorted, but he couldn't get it off.

Before Mother Elephant could come to help him, Little Elephant whirled his trunk around and around in the air. Maybe he could shake it loose.

Suddenly the big wad of taffy flew off and went

He held on and pulled, backing away from his mother

sailing across the room. It landed smack on Grand-pa's wig and kept on going, taking the wig along with it.

Grandpa had been peacefully dozing by the fire. But when he felt his wig suddenly and firmly lifted off, he woke up and clutched his bald head. "Oh me, oh my," he scolded. "There's no peace in this house with Little Elephant around."

Mother Elephant ran to comfort Grandpa and get the taffy out of his wig. Father Elephant didn't know what to say or what to do, so he looked very sternly at Little Elephant and blowing through his trunk, he said, "Humph-ah! Humph-ah!"

But Little Elephant was doubled up with laughter. He had never before seen Grandpa Elephant without his wig. And he *did* look funny!

At last the day was over and everything was quiet. Mother Elephant was knitting and winding off her yarn around Father Elephant's beautifully painted tusks.

Grandpa Elephant was contentedly raking his back with a long-handled scratcher that Mother Elephant had given him for Christmas.

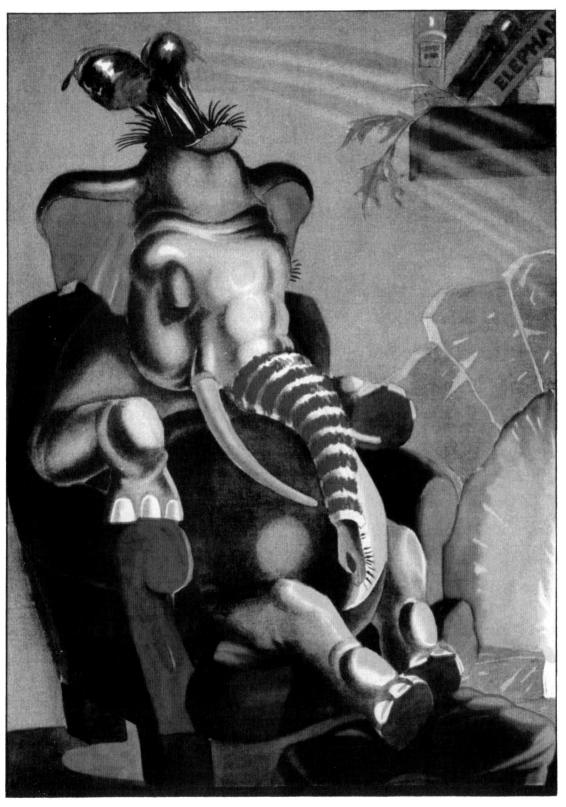

Grandpa had been peacefully dozing by the fire

"A nice Christmas," murmured Mother Elephant.

"Yes, a nice Christmas," nodded Father Elephant sleepily.

"Yes, yes, a very nice Christmas," wheezed Grandpa, giving himself an extra good scratch.

Just then Mother Elephant heard Little Elephant plump into bed. She laid down her knitting and tiptoed upstairs to tell him goodnight. On his pillow lay the big brass trumpet. On his wrist the watch was still ticking away. But Little Elephant was so tired, and so full of dinner and peanuts and popcorn and taffy that he was almost asleep when Mother Elephant tucked in his covers.

As Mother Elephant turned out the lights and closed the door she heard Little Elephant say sleepily, "Gee, that was a nice Christmas."